Gargoylz

Go to a Party

Gargoylz: grotesque stone
creatures found on old
buildings, spouting rainwater
from the guttering.
Sometimes seen causing
mischief and mayhem
before scampering away
over rooftops.

Read all the
Gargoylz adventures!

Gargoylz

Go to a Party

WARRINGTON BOROUGH COUNCIL	
34143100371606	
Bertrams	08/06/2010
JF	£4.99
WOO	

Burchett & Vogler

illustrated by **Leighton Noyes** and **Dynamo Design**

RED FOX

GARGOYLZ GO TO A PARTY
A RED FOX BOOK 978 1 849 41077 9

First published in Great Britain by Red Fox,
an imprint of Random House Children's Books
A Random House Group Company

This edition published 2010

1 3 5 7 9 10 8 6 4 2

Series created and developed by Amber Caravéo
Copyright © Random House Children's Books, 2010
All rights reserved. No part of this publication may be reproduced, stored in
a retrieval system, or transmitted in any form or by any means, electronic,
mechanical, photocopying, recording or otherwise, without the prior permission
of the publishers.
The Random House Group Limited supports the Forest Stewardship Council
(FSC), the leading international forest certification organization. All our titles
that are printed on Greenpeace-approved FSC-certified paper carry the FSC
logo. Our paper procurement policy can be found at
www.rbooks.co.uk/environment

Set in Bembo Schoolbook

Red Fox Books are published by Random House Children's Books,
61–63 Uxbridge Road, London W5 5SA

www.**kids**at**randomhouse**.co.uk
www.**rbooks**.co.uk

Addresses for companies within The Random House Group Limited can be
found at: www.randomhouse.co.uk/offices.htm

THE RANDOM HOUSE GROUP Limited Reg. No. 954009

A CIP catalogue record for this book is available from the British Library.

Printed and bound in Great Britain by CPI Bookmarque, Croydon, CR0 4TD

For Rhiannon Kirk – who has plans for a very special
party with two bouncy castles!
– **Burchett & Vogler**

Hello, I'm the Web Gargoyle.
Look out for me – I'll be hiding in one
of the pictures in the book.
When you spot me, be sure to make a
note of the secret codeword I'm holding.
The codeword unlocks a secret level
of the amazing Gargoylz game
on our fabulous website at
www.gargoylz.co.uk

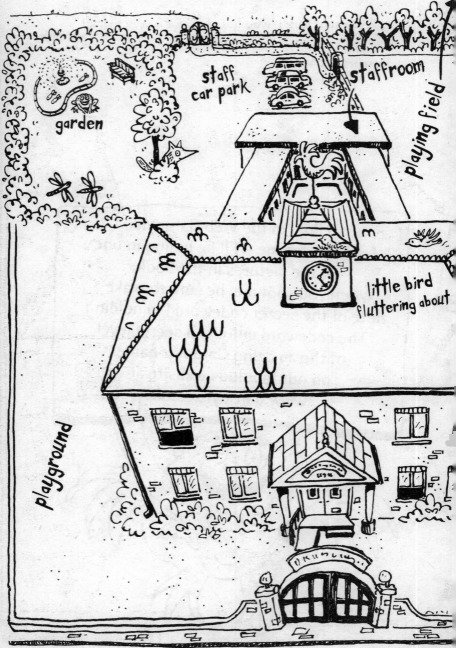

St Mark's Church

playground

squirrel with a yummy nut

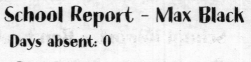

School Report - Max Black

Days absent: 0

Days late: 0

Max is never afraid to make a contribution to history lessons. His demonstration of a battering ram using a broom and a bucket was very realistic, although the resulting hole in the classroom door was not ideal.

I worry that Max only seems to play with Ben Neal, but he assures me he has a lot of friends at the local church.

Class teacher - Miss Deirdre Bleet

Max Black's behaviour this term has been outrageous. He has repeatedly broken school rule number 739: boys must not tell 'knock knock' jokes in assembly. He is still playing pranks with Ben Neal. Mrs Pumpkin is absent again after the exploding paint pot incident. And Mrs Simmer, the head dinner lady, says the mincing machine has never been the same since he fed his maths test into it.

Head teacher - Hagatha Hogsbottom (Mrs)

School Report - Ben Neal

Days absent: 0

Days late: 0

This term Ben has been very inventive in PE. However, attempting to tightrope-walk across the hall was a little dangerous - and used up all the skipping ropes. He spends far too much time in class looking out of the window and waving at the gravestones in the churchyard. He would be better learning his spellings - a word he insists on writing as 'spellingz'.

Class teacher - Miss Deirdre Bleet

Ben Neal is always polite, but I am deeply concerned about his rucksack. It often looks very full - and not with school books, I am certain. It has sometimes been seen to wriggle and squirm. I suspect that he is keeping a pet in there. If so, it is outrageous and there will be trouble.

Head teacher - Hagatha Hogsbottom (Mrs)

Contents

1. Time for a Trick

Ben Neal strapped himself into his
imaginary spy jet pack.

"Ready for liftoff, Agent Black?" he
yelled to his best friend, Max. "We'll be at
school before you can say spaceships!"

"Sorry, Agent Neal," said Max. "I don't
feel like whizzing along today."

"Yeah, I know," said Ben. "It's boring
Monday morning assembly and Mrs
Hogsbottom will be trying to find out
who chucked that beanbag through the
window and into her rice pudding. That
was a brilliant shot of yours."

"True," said
Max, "but
it's not that.
Next Saturday
my stupid little
sister is five and
she's having a pink
princess sleepover
party. My mum and
dad wouldn't talk about
anything else all weekend."

"Bad luck," said Ben
sympathetically.

"I know even girls have to
have birthdays now and again,"
Max went on, "but it was terrible.
They kept going on about whether to
put white or pink sugar fairies on Jessica's
cake and how many of her horrible
friends to invite. Even a top superspy like
me couldn't stand the torture."

"Gruesome!" agreed Ben. "You need

cheering up – let's see if the gargoylz can help."

Ben led the way in through the gates of Oldacre Primary School and over to the wall between the playground and the ancient church next door.

The gargoylz that hung on the church roof were Max and Ben's secret friends. The funny little stone creatures came to life when no other humans were looking, and joined the boys in playing tricks. As the gargoylz had secret powers, the tricks were always spectacular.

"Greetingz!" came a growly purr.

A small stone-coloured

creature was sitting on a gravestone, beaming up at them. It had spiky wings, a face like a monkey's and a dragony tail.

"Hello, Toby," said Max miserably.

"You don't sound very happy," said Toby in surprise.

A round-eyed gargoyle with a spiky ridge down his back popped up from the long grass. "I'll make you laugh," he said. "I could do one of my smells through Mrs Hogsbum's window."

"Could you, Barney?" asked Ben, eyes lighting up.

"Good idea, but it won't help with my

4

problem," said Max. He told the gargoylz about the party plans and the pink princess theme. "I was nearly sick," he complained. "It was pink balloons this and pink icing that. Mum and Dad didn't even come and look when I found a half-eaten bird in the tulips."

"Cool find!" gasped Ben.

"That's what I thought," said Max, brightening up for a moment. "But it got worse. I spent all Sunday training an army of superspy ants to follow a trail of strawberry jam into next door's garage, but when I invited Mum and Dad to see my amazing feat, guess what they said?"

"We'll come at once?" suggested Barney.

"They said they were too busy deciding what shade of pink the princess party bags ought to be!"

"That's disgusting!" said Ben.

"I don't know how I'm going to survive," sighed Max. "It will be the worst girly princess party in the history of worst girly princess parties. And it's at my house. I'm doomed." He slumped against the wall, his head in his hands.

"Will there be cake?" asked Toby.

Max nodded.

The gargoylz' eyes sparkled.

"And cookiez?" added Barney.

"Yes," said Max grumpily. "Pink ones."

The gargoylz rubbed their tummies.

"And there'll be a bouncy castle . . ." Max told them.

"Awesome!" exclaimed Ben.

"Whoopee!" yelled the gargoylz. "We'll come!"

"...but it'll be full of shrieking princesses." Max groaned. "Imagine, a bouncy castle in my own garden — and I won't even get a single bounce on it!" The gargoylz solemnly shook their heads at the dreadful thought.

"I've had an idea, Agent Black," said Ben suddenly. "You can come and stay at my house until the party's over."

7

Max's face broke into a beaming smile. "Good plan, Agent Neal!" he cried in delight. "Why didn't we think of that before?"

"That's all sorted then," said Toby, taking off and dive-bombing the gravestones in his excitement. "Let's celebrate with a good trick."

At that moment the bell rang.

"There's no time now," said Max. "School's starting."

"See you at playtime then," said Toby.

Max fidgeted about at his desk. He couldn't wait to get out into the playground and dream up a new trick with the gargoylz. The lesson had been going on for ever. He was supposed to be writing a poem about a pet he'd like, but nothing seemed to rhyme with tarantula.

"Your turn to read out your work, Max," said a wobbly voice.

His teacher, Miss Bleet, was looking anxiously at him. Miss Bleet always looked anxious when she spoke to Max and Ben. Max could never understand why – after all, they didn't put a beetle in her desk *every* day.

"Er . . ." said Max. "I can't because . . ." As he looked around for an excuse, his eye lit on the clock. It was twenty to eleven. The lesson should have ended ten minutes ago! He looked outside and saw that the other classes were already out in the playground.

"I can't because it's playtime, miss!" said Max, pointing at the clock.

"Oh dear," said Miss Bleet, looking flustered. "I wonder why the bell didn't ring. Er . . . off you go."

Max and Ben led the charge to the door.

"It's not fair," said Ben as they sped down the corridor. "We've hardly got any

break time left to play a trick with the gargoylz."

The boys had just burst out into the playground when they heard a voice.

"The school bell has broken!" it screeched. "So I will be telling you when playtime is over!"

Max turned on his spy radar: grey hair, beaky nose, face like a wrinkled carrot. He knew what that meant. It was Enemy Agent Mrs Hogsbottom, also known as Mrs Hogsbum – codename: Evil Head Teacher.

"PLAYTIME IS OVER!" she bellowed.

"But we've only just got here, Mrs Hogsbu— bottom," protested Max.

"And we must have our exercise," said Ben, flashing his blue eyes hopefully

12

at her. This always worked on the dinner ladies, who gave him extra sprinkles on his sponge cake. It never worked on Mrs Hogsbottom.

"Outrageous!" shouted the furious head teacher. "School rule number five hundred and fourteen — boys will not take advantage of the bell not working."

She pointed at the door and the boys didn't dare argue any more.

"I hope that bell gets mended soon," said Max as they mooched back into their classroom. "I don't think I can put up with Mrs Hogsbum blaring like a foghorn a zillion times a day."

"I've just had a terrible thought," said Ben. "What if Miss Bleet doesn't keep an eye on the clock and we're late for lunch too? I don't think I could survive all that extra learning!"

"Don't worry, Agent Neal." Max winked at him. "I've been thinking about that and I have a plan – Secret Plan: Clock Watch."

"Excellent, Agent Black," said Ben. "How does it work?"

"We take turns to watch the clock – five-minute shifts," explained Max. "Then we can tell Miss Bleet the moment it's time for lunch. I'll have first go."

The next lesson was maths. Ben joined up the sums in his book into an elephant shape while Max kept his eyes firmly fixed on the clock. After a while he gave Ben a nudge.

"The clock's gone wrong like the bell," he said. "I must have been looking at it for hours but the hand's only gone round three and a half minutes."

Ben checked his watch. "I'm afraid the clock's right," he said. "But at this rate we'll starve to death by lunch time."

Max put his head down on the desk. "This day's going from bad to worse," he groaned.

"Don't worry," said Ben. "I've just had an awesome idea for a brilliant trick."

"Tell me more," said Max, perking up immediately.

They ducked down behind their calculators and began to whisper.

Lunch time came at last – ten minutes late. The boys had been so busy devising their trick they'd forgotten to keep an eye on the clock.

They ate their dinner at record speed and raced over to the wall by the church.

Toby flew down to perch next to them and Barney scrambled up to join him.

"Have I got a prank for you!" declared Ben. "The school bell's broken and Miss Bleet keeps having to look at the clock to see when the lessons are over."

"But she's hopeless at it," said Max, "so we keep getting extra education!"

"That's horrible," said Barney with a shudder.

"We thought maybe you gargoylz could sneak inside during afternoon play and put all the clocks forward by fifteen minutes," said Ben. "Then we'll get to go home early!"

"Soundz fun," said Toby. "But why wait? We'll do it now."

"No, it's too risky," said Max. "A teacher is sure to notice if we do it too soon."

Toby nodded. "Afternoon playtime it is then."

"Brilliant," said Ben. "We'll do the clock in our classroom. The rest is up to you."

"You can count on us," said Barney as the two gargoylz happily scampered away to tell their friends.

When Miss Bleet announced afternoon playtime – two minutes late – Max dragged Ben over to look at Harry, the class gerbil. "Pretend we're talking to him," Max whispered.

18

"As soon as Miss Bleet's gone, we'll do the clock."

Ben watched as their teacher went off for her coffee. "Coast's clear!" he hissed.

Max jumped up, dragged a chair over to the clock and moved the minute hand forwards by a quarter of an hour.

Then, trying to look innocent, they sauntered out into the playground and over to the churchyard wall.

"Let's see how the gargoylz are getting on with the trick," said Ben.

"Ahoy there, shipmates!" came a
loud squawk.

A gargoyle was perched
on the wall. It was Ira. He
looked a bit like a parrot
and a bit like an eagle
and liked to think he
was a fierce pirate.
He was holding a
telescope to his eye
and scanning the
playground.

"Are you the lookout?"
asked Max.

"Aye-aye," said Ira. "I've borrowed
the vicar's spyglass. I'm checking that my
crew makes it safely back from changing
the clocks."

Suddenly he flapped a wing towards
the school building. "Gargoyle on the
horizon!" he squawked.

A grass snake was slithering out of the

Reception class window and up into the gutter. Then it changed into a gargoyle with a head full of wriggling snakes, and scuttled towards them.

"That's Eli finished," said Max.

"And Theo," added Ben as a cute little kitten jumped out of a Year Four classroom window and sat on the windowsill to wash its paws. Some girls tried to pick it up and the kitten immediately let out a miaow of alarm and fled. Once over the playground wall, it turned back into a gargoyle again.

"I had to get away," said Theo. "I didn't want to scare the girlz with my fierce teeth and clawz," he explained.

Theo's special power was turning into a fearsome tiger, but as he was a very young gargoyle – just four hundred and twelve years old – he only ever managed to become a soft, fluffy kitten.

Toby flew down from the school roof. "Greetingz!" he purred. "I've changed the clocks in the Year Three and Year One classrooms. Dangling drainpipes! I haven't had so much fun since we made the vicar's watch go backwardz and he had breakfast twice!"

Pop! Zack appeared out of thin air next to them. "Done Year Two!" he said, shaking his mane excitedly. "Done Year Two!"

"Just Barney to come back into port!" squawked Ira. "He's doing all the other classes."

"I can't see him," said Max. "But I can see Mrs Hogsbum!"

"Everybody in!" screeched the head teacher from the other side of the playground.

"If Barney doesn't hurry, he's going to be trapped!" said Ben, looking worried. "Which classroom is he in?"

"That one," said Toby, pointing.

"That's my sister's class," said Ben. "They've got a spelling test next."

"Poor Barney," sighed Max. "That's a fate worse than death!"

"Hurry up, children!" yelled Mrs Hogsbottom. Her piercing eyes were sweeping the playground like evil laser beams.

"She'll see us at any moment," groaned Max. "But we can't go in till we know Barney's safe."

"There he blows!" squawked Ira.

Barney was belting across the staffroom roof. He slid down the drainpipe and launched himself over the churchyard wall. His doggy face looked terrified and there were red and green splodges all over his cheeks.

24

"Teacher came in," he panted. "Nearly got caught! Had to hide in the paints."

"Did you do the clock?" asked Ben. Barney nodded. Then he grinned proudly. "And before that I sneaked into Mrs Hogsbum's room and let off my secret power, like I said I would. She soon came racing out to get away from the stink. Then, while she was gone, I put her clock forward too!"

"Awesome prank, Barney!" said Ben.

"Max and Ben!" shrieked the head teacher. "You'll be seeing me in my office if you don't go to your class at once!" The boys fled inside.

★ ★ ★

Max and Ben sat in their classroom, trying not to laugh too loudly.

"This is an awesome prank," said Max, sneaking a look up at the clock. "It's only twenty minutes until home time."

"I hope no one notices the time's wrong," said Ben. "This is so exciting. We can spend ages with the gargoylz after school." He wriggled in his chair with excitement.

"What's wrong, Ben?" called Miss Bleet.

The class looked up from their pictures of the solar system.

"He's got ants in his pants!" tittered Lucinda Tellingly, and the class sniggered.

"Of course I haven't!" protested Ben, embarrassed. He tried to concentrate on his drawing of Saturn, which was looking more like a fried egg than a planet. In the end he gave up and drew a sausage to go with it.

"Ten minutes left!" hissed Max, bouncing on his seat and sending his colouring pencils flying.

"Max Black!" sighed Miss Bleet. "Do you need to go to the toilet?"

Lucinda, Poppy and Tiffany giggled. Max went pink and shook his head. "I must sit still," he muttered to himself. "I must sit still."

"Help me finish my picture," Ben told him. "That'll take your mind off the time."

Max looked at Ben's book. "It doesn't look much like Saturn," he said doubtfully.

"It's not," said Ben. "It's breakfast. You can colour in the baked beans."

Max had just finished the last bean when he noticed the clock. "Awesome!" he yelled at the top of his voice. "It's home time, miss."

"But it feels like we've only just started," murmured Miss Bleet, staring at the clock in disbelief. "Oh well, you'd better go then."

Max and Ben grabbed their
rucksacks and sprinted along
the corridor, dodging the
other people pouring
out of their classrooms.
They were almost at
the school gates when
they heard a bellow
from behind them.

"Outrageous!"

"It's Mrs Hogsbum,"
shouted Max. "Hide!" The
boys whizzed into the churchyard
and threw themselves down behind
the wall. They peeped back over into
the playground. The older juniors were
happily racing off through the school
gates as their red-faced head teacher
stormed out of the school buildings and
began to round up the younger children
like a hyperactive sheepdog.

"Outrageous!" she screeched. "School's

not over yet! Everyone stay here until your parents arrive. But there will be no running, no skipping and no noisy games."

"Our classroom clock said it was home time," piped up a brave girl from Year Two.

"My watch says you still have thirteen minutes and forty-seven seconds of school left," snapped Mrs Hogsbottom, "and my watch is always right."

"That's something even the gargoylz wouldn't dare change," whispered Max.

"We weren't going near that monster," came a growl, and Toby flew down next to them.

"I don't blame you," said Ben. "No one goes near her without full armour and earplugs."

"Thank you, gargoylz," said Max. "Now we've got ages to play with you."

"And I know the perfect game," said Toby with a huge grin. "Let's play What's the Time, Mr Wolf?"

2. Hide-and-Seek

Der-ring! Max's doorbell rang loudly.

"I'll get it!" Max called to his mother.
"It'll be Ben and his mum. They've come
to sort out my sleepover at his house." He
slid down the banister and flung open his
front door.

"It's Friday!" he yelled. "Just school to
get through today and then it's our great
escape weekend!" He suddenly noticed
Ben's downturned mouth. "What's up,
Agent Neal?" he asked as his mum took
Mrs Neal off into the lounge. "You look
like you've bitten into an apple and found

half a maggot."

"Disaster, Agent Black!" groaned Ben. "We can't sleep at my house after all. Mum and Dad are going on a walking trip. My mum's asking yours if I can stay here instead!"

Max's eyes were wide with horror. "But what about Jessica's party?" he croaked. "The house will be full of frilly, screaming girls. It'll be a nightmare!"

"I told Mum and Dad that," said Ben gloomily. "But they reckoned it would be fun and we could help out."

"We'll be serving jelly and ice cream to yucky pink princesses," predicted Max.

"Or winning some horrible doll in Pass
the Parcel," added Ben.

"And I bet they'll make us dress up!"
said Max. "We'll never survive!"

The two mums came out of the lounge.
Mrs Neal was telling Mrs Black all about
the boots and fleeces and thick socks she'd
had to buy for their exciting walking trip.

"What a waste of money!" Ben whispered to Max. "They could have bought a really cool skateboard instead."

"Grown-ups have funny ideas sometimes," said Max pityingly. Then his face brightened. "We're off to school, Mum," he yelled, grabbing Ben and shoving him out of the front door.

"What are you up to?" demanded Ben.

"Climb aboard the spymobile!" ordered Max, revving up the imaginary vehicle at the gate. "I've thought of an idea to get us out of sleeping at my house. On our way to school we'll ask Secret Agent Nan if we can stay with her instead."

"Brilliant plan!" exclaimed Ben.

"Problem solved – and we'll get plenty of yummy food."

They were soon knocking at Max's grandmother's front door.

The door opened. Max's spy radar went into action: curly hair, big smile, flowery dressing gown. Max knew what that meant. It was Nan – codename: Supercook.

"How nice to see you, boys," she said. "Come in. I've got some cookies you can take to school with you."

The boys' eyes grew as round as saucers and they immediately forgot why they were there. "Cor, thanks, Nan," said Max as they trooped after her into the kitchen.

It was only when they were setting off down the path again, their mouths full of delicious, crumbly cookies, that Max suddenly stopped, a horrified expression on his face. "Our mission, Agent Neal!" he gasped, spitting crumbs all over his grandmother's roses.

"It was the cookies' fault we forgot," said Ben. "They were too scrumptious."

The boys scampered back to the door and explained their dreadful plight to Max's nan.

"So you see," Max said, finishing their sorry tale, "we need to be rescued from a party full of pink princesses. Can we stay with you?"

To their dismay Nan shook her head. "I'd love to say yes, dear," she said, "but I'm off on a trip to Norway with my karate club. We leave this afternoon."

"I can't believe it!" said Max in disgust as the boys mooched in the school gates a few minutes later. "Nans are supposed to stay at home and do baking and stuff, not trot off round the world chopping up bricks with their bare hands."

"Perhaps we should change her codename from Supercook to Action Nan," said Ben grimly.

"Greetingz!" Toby leaped down onto the church wall, beaming from ear to ear.

Zack appeared next to him with a **pop!** "Time for a trick! Time for a trick!" he chanted, mane quivering with excitement.

"We don't feel like playing tricks," said Max. He explained that there was no way they could get out of being at Jessica's party.

Zack hung over the wall making sicky noises at the terrible thought.

38

"Dangling drainpipes! That's serious," said Toby. "But I've got an idea. When the vicar wanted to clean the church gutterz, we hid his ladder."

"Cool trick," said Ben. Then he frowned. "But that's no good to us. Mum and Dad aren't cleaning gutters."

"No, you doughnut!" exclaimed Max. "Toby's just giving us an example. Your parents are going walking, so we hide all their walking gear. Then they can't go."

"Brilliant!" cried Ben. "We'll be able to sleep round mine and escape the dreaded party after all."

"We'll help," said Zack, hopping into Ben's rucksack. "Let's go now."

"We can't," laughed Ben, tipping the wriggling gargoyle out over the church wall before anyone saw him.

"We've got to go to school—"

"Outrageous!" came a shriek.

Toby hopped smartly out of sight as the boys turned to see an angry Mrs Hogsbottom wagging a finger at them from her office window.

"Ben Neal, you have broken school rule number seven hundred and forty-three. Boys must not shake their rucksacks over church walls. Get to your class immediately!"

THIS IS TO CERTIFY THAT MRS HOGSBOTTOM SHOUTS A LOT Signed

"Don't worry, gargoylz," Ben whispered. "You can come and help us after school. I'm sure we'll need you!" And he ran off to his classroom with Max.

The boys couldn't wait for school to finish. Unfortunately the school bell had been mended so they couldn't trick their way out of class early today. However, as soon as the bell went, they zoomed out of the door, sending Miss Bleet into a spin. Toby and Zack were waiting for them behind a gravestone in the churchyard, jigging with excitement.

Toby zipped himself
into Max's rucksack.
Zack waggled a wing
at Ben.

"No tipping this
time!" he warned,
rubbing his bottom.
"Landed on a
prickle this morning."
"Don't worry,
though," came Toby's
muffled voice. "You know he
loves pricklz. He gobbled it all up before I
could get any."

The boys sped off to Ben's house to find
his mum and dad rushing up and down
the hall, stuffing their last few clothes into
bulging backpacks.

"How can we hide their walking stuff?"
wondered Max. "They'll notice if we run
off with their bags."

"Good spies are always on the alert,"

Ben told him. "We'll find a way."

"Why do grown-ups make such a fuss about things?" said Max as Mr Neal shot past with an armful of umbrellas. "All they need is pyjamas and a toothbrush."

Ben's mum burst out of the kitchen and threw two pairs of walking boots onto the pile of torches, maps and cameras. "I've packed your bag for the weekend," she told Ben.

"He won't be needing that!" Toby piped up cheekily from Max's rucksack.

"Pardon, Max?" said Mrs Neal.

"I said . . . he won't be needing a hat," answered Max quickly.

Mrs Neal gave him a puzzled look and went upstairs again.

"Keep quiet in there," Max hissed over his shoulder.

Ben's dad wandered past tapping his pockets. "Where have I put them . . . ?" he muttered. "Gwendoline," he called, "have you seen the car keys?" He started rummaging through a box of shoes.

Ben spotted a glint of metal next to the phone. His eyes lit up. "Secret Plan: Hide the Keys," he whispered to Max, pointing to the keys.

While Ben's dad rifled through his briefcase, Max snatched up the keys and dropped them in the plant pot by the door.

"Keys hidden," he reported in Ben's ear. "Now your parents can't go. We can stay here. Party avoided!"

"Mission accomplished," Ben agreed. There were muffled cheers from the rucksacks. But then Ben's mum flew down the stairs, two at a time. To the boys' dismay she was carrying some car keys.

"We haven't got time to look for your keys now," she told Ben's dad. "We'll use the spare ones instead."

Max and Ben groaned inwardly. Mrs Neal thrust Ben's bag into his hand and shooed the boys towards the door. "Wait for us in the car."

"But we can't!" exclaimed Ben in horror. "Er, I mean . . . it looks like you need our help."

"Help?" came Toby's growly voice. "That's not what we're here for."

"What was that, Max?" asked Mrs Neal.

"I said . . . help? That's *just* what we're here for," gabbled Max, giving the rucksack a nudge.

"I just need to check if the fleeces are dry and then we'll be off," Mrs Neal muttered to herself.

Ben's face lit up. "I've got an idea," he hissed to Max. "Get into the garden! Turbo-speed!"

"I just want to say goodbye to the climbing frame," he told his mum as he and Max dashed past her and out of the back door.

They hid behind a holly bush.

"Toby, Zack, we need you," Ben called into the rucksacks. The two eager gargoylz popped out.

"Reporting for duty," said Toby, giving a salute.

"See those yellow fleeces on the washing line?" Ben asked him. "Toby, I want you to put them in the apple tree – as high as you can."

"No problem!" declared Toby, scampering off. Soon he was flying up to the top of the apple tree like a bird, the fleeces in his teeth.

"We're doing Mum and Dad a favour really," Ben told Max as they watched Toby drape the fluffy jackets over the highest branch. "They shouldn't have even been thinking of wearing bright yellow fleeces. They'd look like bananas."

"I want to help!
I want to help!"
demanded Zack.

"Don't worry,"
said Max. "I've
thought of
something very
important for you
to do. Take out the
shoelaces." He jumped
up in alarm as Zack dived
for his trainers. "No, not mine! The
ones in the boots Ben's parents are taking
on their trip. They're in the hall."

Pop! In an instant Zack had vanished.

"Good one, Agent Black!" exclaimed
Ben. "We're definitely safe from the perils
of the pink party now."

"Let's see how Zack's getting on," said
Max happily.

They spun round and bumped straight
into Mrs Neal.

"How did they get up there?" she demanded, pointing at the fleeces.

"There was a tornado," Ben told her.

"We were lucky we escaped," added Max.

Ben's mother stared at them suspiciously for a moment. Then she rolled up her sleeves and began to climb the apple tree. Just in time, Toby flew out and dived back into a rucksack.

"Foiled again," sighed Max.

"Let's hope Zack's carried out his plan," said Ben as they went back inside. "He's our last hope."

The boots lay in the hall.

"No laces," said Max. "But where's Zack?"

Toby scrambled out of the rucksack and they looked around.

"Over there," gasped Ben.

The end of a brown bootlace was sticking out from the door of the cupboard under the stairs. Ben flung it open. Inside was a wriggling bundle of laces.

"Is that you, Zack?" said Ben.

Pop! Zack appeared in the middle of the tangle.

"You look like an Egyptian mummy!" Toby burst out as the boys began to unwrap him.

"You've done an excellent job, Zack," said Ben, helping to untie the wriggling gargoyle. "Mum and Dad won't be going anywhere without their boots so we can start the sleepover now. Let's go to my room."

Once Zack was free, they all tore up the stairs. Ben got out his pirate ship and they set sail across his bedroom carpet.

"Landlubberz ahoy!" yelled Toby, perched on the deck. He grinned at the boys. "Wait till I tell Ira I was a pirate. I haven't had this much fun since we put

soap flakes in the vicar's porridge and he
foamed at the mouth."

"Cleaned his teeth! Cleaned his teeth!"
declared Zack happily.

"Ben, Max!" Mrs Neal's voice drifted
up the stairs. "Time to go."

The boys and gargoylz gawped at each
other.

"That's not possible," gasped Ben.
"What's happened?"

They went out and peered over the
banisters.

Mr and Mrs Neal were standing in the hall. Their yellow fleeces were covered in leaves, there was a mouldy apple sticking out of one pocket and their boots were laced with string – but they were ready.

"I don't believe it," groaned Ben. "All our plans have failed."

Max turned to the gargoylz. "Quick, escape through Ben's bedroom window," he said, "otherwise you'll have to come with us into the pink house of horror."

"You wouldn't catch us there!" declared Toby, flying off.

"No chance!" added Zack, sliding down the drainpipe.

The boys went down to the car. As it pulled away, they saw the gargoylz waving merrily at them from the porch roof.

Max's mum was sitting at the kitchen table with Jessica, busy stuffing pink sparkly things into bright party bags.

"You're just in time to help," said Mrs

Black when she saw the boys. She shoved
a pile of plastic hair slides across the table.
"Put one in each bag, please."

"We're doomed, Agent Neal," hissed
Max.

They slumped down on the other
chairs.

"What long faces!" laughed Max's
mum. "But I've got something to cheer
you up."

"You haven't done pink party bags for
us, have you?" asked Max in alarm.

"No," said Jessica firmly. "Boys don't deserve party bags."

"It's not frilly pink outfits, is it?" asked Ben in horror.

Max's mum shook her head. "As the house will be full of princesses tomorrow," – the boys shuddered – "Dad's going to put the tent up at the bottom of the garden for tomorrow night. You and Ben can sleep down there, away from the party."

"Awesome!" yelled Max. He jumped up and high-fived with Ben, scattering the hair slides all over the floor. "Can Dad put the tent up now?"

"He's too busy pinning up the flags in the front garden,"

said Mum. "He'll do it in the morning."

Max and Ben picked up the hair slides and began shoving them happily into the party bags.

"I never thought I'd say this," said Ben, "but I can't wait for the princess party to start!"

3. Pink Princess Peril!

"Wheeeeeeeee!"

Max sat bolt upright in his bed wondering what the ear-splitting noise was. He'd been having a lovely dream. Toby had taught him to fly and he'd been dive-bombing Mrs Hogsbum.

"Wasss going on?" demanded a sleepy voice.

Max leaned over the edge of his bed. He could just see Ben's tangled blond hair peeping out from his sleeping bag. "It's coming from downstairs," he told him.

"Sounds like a piglet that's sat on a

pin," grumbled Ben.

"Let's investigate, Agent Neal," suggested Max.

They followed the dreadful screeching down to the lounge.

Jessica was sitting in the middle of the carpet surrounded by pink, shiny wrapping paper. "I'm five!" she squealed. "Look at all my presents!"

Max and Ben
tried to shield their
eyes from the
singing dolls,
fluffy woodland
creatures
and sparkly
hairbands strewn
around the floor.

Max's mum
came in from the
kitchen. "You could
have waited for us, Jess,"
she said. Then she saw the
boys pretending to be sick in the
corner. "That's enough, you two!"

Jessica stuck her tongue out at them
behind her mother's back.

"Haven't you got something to say to
Jessica, Max?" said Mrs Black.

"Happy birthday," muttered Max.

"And your present?" hissed his mother.

"Oh, that!" Max plodded upstairs and pulled out the pink-wrapped parcel from under his bed. His mum had made it look all girly, with ribbons and glitter, but it had got nicely squashed when the boys had played Spy Trampoline on the bed last night. Max blew off the dust, ran back downstairs and thrust it at his sister.

"Here you are," he mumbled. "It was the best one in the shop."

Jessica tore it open. It was a jigsaw with a T. rex eating a Triceratops on it.

"Cool!" said Ben admiringly.

"Yuck!" declared Jessica, throwing it on the floor.

"What do you say, Jessica?" prompted her mother.

"Thanks," grunted Jessica.

Ben held out his present. Jessica took it and unwrapped it. "A pink pony!" she shrieked in delight. "So pretty! Wait till I show my friends."

"My mum chose it, not me," Ben told her, backing away in horror and stepping on her new Terence the Talking Turtle, which began to recite a poem about pixies.

All morning Max and Ben tried to keep out of the way of the party preparations. It wasn't easy: the kitchen was crammed with party plates and napkins, the lounge was stuffed with Jessica's new toys, and Mum was sticking pink streamers and balloons up all over the place.

"The only safe room is the toilet!" Max complained to Ben after lunch. "I'm getting allergic to pink. We need to escape from all this girly birthday stuff."

"Good idea, Agent Black," said Ben. "Time for Secret Plan: Prepare Rucksacks. Your dad's put up the tent. Let's go and hide away in our spy camp at the bottom of the garden."

"Last one there is a sausage!" yelled Max.

Ten minutes later, their rucksacks stuffed with essential equipment, the boys bounded into the garden and nearly crashed into Mr Black. He was fiddling with a huge round bundle wrapped in a tarpaulin.

"The bouncy castle's arrived," he told them.

"We'll help put it up!" offered Max. "Then we can test it out before the princesses come."

Dad switched on the motor. "Soon have it blown up," he said cheerily. He pulled away the covering and the castle slowly filled with air and took shape in front of them.

"Oh, no!" gasped Max.
"It's PINK!"
"*Very* pink," agreed Ben
weakly as a pink turret popped up
into the air, with a jaunty pink flag at
the top.
"*Totally* pink!" croaked Max.

The castle stood majestically on its base. It had four towers entwined with pretty painted roses, and glowed bright pink in the sun.

The boys shuddered.

SECRET CODEWORD: GAME

"Hideous!" declared Ben. "It's more of a pink palace than a bouncy castle. If we go on that, the colour will blind us."

"Too right," agreed Max. "Escape to the spy camp!"

They sprinted for the tent, which Max's dad had set up among the trees at the bottom of the garden. It had been Max's granddad's when he was a boy, and it was big, brown and sturdy.

"I've got all the comics and games," said Ben, pulling out his latest electronic game.

"And I've got the joke books and the action figures," said Max, spilling his bursting bag onto the groundsheet.

Ben and Max had just finished level seven of Attack of the Killer Courgettes when horrible screeches filled the air.

Max peeped out of the tent. His spy radar was fizzing: shriekingly loud, extremely annoying, sparkly crown bobbing up above the pink inflatable turrets. He knew what that meant. It was Enemy Agent Jessica Black, codename: Disgusting Little Sister. And she was surrounded by her annoying friends on the bouncy castle.

"Enemy agents on the loose," said Ben. "They're swarming all over the pink palace."

"Let's set up a Superspy Warning System," suggested Max. "Then we'll know if they come near."

"Good thinking," said Ben.

"If we tie a row of tin cans across the garden," said Max, "anyone who comes down here will run into it and make a terrible clatter."

He fetched an armful of tins from the recycling and some string. "Now we just need the washing line." He pulled out a

pair of scissors and was soon back with a
trailing length of red plastic cord, pegs still
attached.

They tied each can to a piece of string
and pegged the cans-on-strings to the
washing line in a long jangly row. Then
they each took one end of the line and
stretched it across the garden.

"I'll fix this end to the trellis," said Ben.

"And I'll tie this end to a tree," said Max.

They stood back to admire their Superspy Warning System as it stretched across the end of the garden at knee height, hidden by the long grass.

"Anyone approaching will definitely set off the alarm, Agent Black," said Ben proudly.

"And the minute we hear it, Agent Neal," said Max with a wink, "we let fly our secret weapon."

He dragged a bucket full of water and several big gloopy sponges out from behind the tent. "Mum and Dad left this here after they washed the garden chairs," he said. "I thought it might come in useful."

"Awesome!" exclaimed Ben. "I hope some nosy girls come along! They'll run straight into our water ambush."

Back inside the tent, Max opened the joke book. "Now for some more fun." He turned the pages. "Here's a good one. What do you call a dinosaur with only one eye?"

"I don't know," said Ben. "What do you call a dinosaur with only one eye?"

"A Do-you-think-he-saurus!" The boys roared with laughter.

Jangle, jingle, jangle!

Ben stopped laughing. "That's the alarm."

"Someone's coming," said Max.

He unzipped the tent opening a little and they peered out.

Max's jaw dropped. A pointy red hat with a pink veil fluttering from the top was bobbing along through the long grass. The tin cans clanged wildly.

"Is it one of the girls?" whispered Ben.
"She's very short."

They crept out of the tent and grabbed
a wet sponge each.

"Ready . . . aim . . . fire!" yelled Max.

The boys launched their dripping
missiles, which hit the hat with a splat.

"Bull's-eye!" cried Ben.

"Spluttering gutterz!" shouted their
victim as he came into view.

Max's spy radar jumped into action:
monkey face, big pointy ears, flapping

wings. He knew what that meant. It was
Toby. But their little friend was
in disguise! The princess hat
was tied under his chin
with a bit of tinsel and
he wore a sparkly belt
round his tummy.

"Sponges down,"
ordered Max quickly.

"Sorry, Toby," said
Ben, rushing over and
drying him off with his
T-shirt. "We thought you were
a gruesome girl."

"I'm a princess," said Toby indignantly.
"Can't you see? This is the hat your nan
plonked on my head when she thought I
was a garden gnome. I just made it pinker
and prettier."

"But why do you want to be a
princess?" asked Max, horrified. "We're
overrun with princesses as it is."

"It's a princess party, isn't it?" explained
Toby. He gave a loud whistle. The
long grass rippled and the cans
clattered together, making
a terrible din, as six more
gargoylz appeared.
"We're *all* princesses!"
growled Cyrus proudly.
Max and Ben gawped
at them. Cyrus had a
sparkly tiara perched
between his pointy ears.
Rufus wore a satin bridesmaid's
dress stretched over his large frame,
and Barney was shuffling along in pink
fluffy slippers. Zack was dashing about
wrapped in a pink lace curtain. It was
too long, and each time he tripped, he
accidentally vanished with a **pop!**
"Look at Bart!" gasped Ben.
The grumpy little gargoyle wore a
shiny petticoat over his gladiator skirt.

"At least I don't look like a toilet brush," he said sulkily, pointing at Theo.

"I don't look like a toilet brush. I look lovely," insisted Theo. He had a pink ballet tutu around his stripy middle and a bow tied to one ear.

Shrieking with laughter, Max and Ben rolled about on the grass.

"I don't see what's so funny!" huffed Toby.

The gargoylz were standing in a line, paws on hips, faces frowning out from their pink costumes. Max and Ben laughed even harder.

"We got the costumes ourselves," said Barney, sounding a little hurt. "From the church charity box."

"It's a very clever idea!" said Max quickly.

"And you all look wonderful," added Ben.

The gargoylz beamed happily.

Pop! Zack disappeared, although his pink lace curtain could still be seen zooming towards the tent. "Where are the cookiez and cakes?" he asked.

"Good point," said Rufus. "It's a party, and partiez are meant to have yummy food."

"There's lots of party food," explained Max, "but—"

"Can we have some then?" Theo interrupted.

"There's a problem," Max went on. "The feast is inside, and the only way to get to it is past the pink palace" – his voice dropped to a horrified whisper – "and that's full of girls."

"I'll go! I'll go!" declared Zack, popping into view. "They won't see me."

"But will you be able to stay invisible when you're faced with pizza and chocolate cake and iced biscuits?" asked Ben. "You know humans mustn't see you."

"Of course!" said Zack.

"No you won't!" chorused the others.

"You always get too excited," grumbled Bart.

"And anyway, your costume will still show," Cyrus added.

"Well, how are we going to get to the food then?" asked Toby.

Max and Ben looked at each other. "We'll have to take on this dangerous mission ourselves, Agent Neal," said Max.

"You'll need a disguise," said Barney, taking off his fluffy pink slippers. "Put these on, Max. Lend him your curtain, Zack."

"I'm not wearing those!" said Max in alarm.

"You have no choice," said Bart sternly.

"He's right," sighed Ben. "Pass me your dress, Rufus."

He put on the dress and, swiping the veil from Toby's hat, draped it over his face. "Princess Ben at your service," he trilled, giving a wobbly curtsy.

The gargoylz burst out laughing.

Max plonked Toby's hat on and tied the lacy curtain round his waist. "This is a serious mission," he told the giggling gargoylz. "Ben and I are going deep into enemy territory. We may not make it back without being shrieked at – or, worse, laughed at – by a whole load of five-year-old girls."

"Which way shall we go?" asked Ben.

"Over the rockery, behind the runner beans and under the bird table," said Max. "Then we'll take cover behind the dustbins before the final dash. After that it's down the side path to the front door. No one will be expecting that. We can join the line of princesses waiting to come in. Jessica's invited thousands so there's sure to be some still arriving."

Max and Ben set off. They stepped
carefully over their tin-can alarm system
and skipped across to the rockery like little
princesses. Soon they were peering round
the corner of the
house into the
front garden.

A line of
excited five-year-
olds in princess
costumes stretched
away from the
front door.

"Good," said Max. "It's Dad at the
door. He won't notice it's us."

"Let's go!" hissed Ben.

They trotted out from their hiding
place and joined the back of the queue. As
they went past Dad, they kept their heads
down.

"Nice frock," said Mr Black as Ben
slunk past.

The boys zoomed into the lounge.
Every centimetre of the room
was covered in sparkly
pink decorations.

"It's so girly!"
gasped Ben. "It's
enough to make
a superspy
collapse with
pink poisoning."

"We have to
brave it," said
Max grimly,
"or starve."

Pushing aside
the pink streamers
and balloons, they
made for the table.
Fantastic food filled
every space.

"Look at this feast!"
said Max. "Doughnuts,

cookies, crisps, sausage rolls.
I don't know where to
start."

Ben grabbed some
chocolate fingers
and cheese sticks.
"How are we going
to carry this?" he
asked suddenly.
"We haven't got
any pockets."

Max held the
lace curtain out
in front of him.
"This makes a
great food sling,"
he said. Ben did
the same with the
bridesmaid's dress.
They filled their skirts
with goodies at mega
spy-speed.

"Let's get back to the gargoylz," said
Max, waddling towards the door. "We'll
take the kitchen route."

They crept into the hall. It was empty.
So far, so good.

But they had just got to the kitchen
door when a horrible shrill squeal filled
the air.

"**Aaaaaaaaaaah!**"

The boys spun round.
Jessica was standing by
the stairs.

"Max and Ben
are princesses!" she
mocked. "Max
and Ben are
princesses!"

All at once
the hall was full
of screaming
girls, laughing
at them.

Max thought he would explode with the horror of it all. He and Ben had to escape — and quickly. He thought hard. "Oooh!" he cried in a silly voice. "What a lovely fluffy-wuffy little kitten! It just ran upstairs."

At once the girls gave chase in a squealing swarm.

"RUN, BEN!" yelled Max.

The boys didn't stop until they'd reached the tent.

"That fooled them," said Ben.

"And we didn't lose a single iced bun."

The tent flap opened and Bart peered out. "Hurry up out there," he said grumpily. "We're hungry."

The boys spilled the feast onto the tent floor. The cakes were a bit squashed and mixed up with the crisps, but the gargoylz fell on them.

"Mmm!" said Ben, munching a sausage roll covered in sprinkles. "This is a great combination."

"It's the best feast I've had since we nibbled all the vicar's scones and he thought he had mice," said Toby.

"I like princess parties," said Barney happily.

"If a princess party means a fantastic feast in a tent with your friends, then so do I!" declared Max.

4. Party Time!

"Dangling drainpipes!" said Toby, rubbing his round belly. "That was a fine feast."

"We've been eating and reading comics for ages," said Ben, peeping out through the tent flap. "It's getting dark outside."

"Bouncy castle time! Bouncy castle time!" yelled Zack, jumping all over the boys' sleeping bags.

Girly shrieks echoed across the garden.

"Enemy Agent Princesses still awake and noisy," Ben reported.

"We'll have to wait until they've gone inside," said Max.

"I want to go and bounce now," grunted Bart. He burped up some grumpy-looking spiders.

"We've been stuck in this smelly old tent all afternoon."

"But you might be seen," warned Ben. "And if there's one thing worse than being seen by ordinary humans, it's being seen by screechy girls."

"We'll play a guessing game to pass the time," said Max. He switched on his torch and made a shadow shape on the side of the tent. "What's this?" he asked, waggling two fingers above his clenched fist.

The gargoylz watched the shadow on the canvas.

"It's a fork!" shouted Bart.

"Is it a hedgehog?" asked Theo.

"It's the vicar!" cried Barney.

"It was meant to be a rabbit," sighed Max. "Ben, you try one."

Ben bent his wrist and straightened his fingers to make a beak.

"Worm!" yelled Zack.

"Snake!" cried Eli.

"You're all wrong," said Bart. "Anyone can see it's a penguin."

"Actually, it's a swan," said Ben.

"Maybe this isn't such a good game . . ." sighed Max.

Jingle, jangle, jingle!

"There goes the alarm," hissed Ben. "I can hear giggling. Girl Attack!"

"Princess Max . . . Princess Ben . . ."
came Jessica's voice.

"Get the sponges, Agent Neal," said
Max. Then he stopped. "No, wait, I've had
a better idea – Secret Plan: Scare the Girls
into the House."

"Leaving the bouncy castle for us!"
exclaimed Toby.

"About time too," muttered Bart.

"First we'll lure them over with some
sickly sweet shadow shapes," said Max
with a mischievous grin. "And then, when
they're right outside, we'll show them
some really scary ones!"

"Start with the rabbit," said
Ben.

Max wiggled his fingers
in front of the torch beam.
"Ooohhh!" they
heard one of Jessica's
friends say. "Look at
the cute bunny."

94

"That's so sweet," came another shrill voice.

"Yuck!" whispered Max. He put his hands together to make wings and fluttered his fingers.

"It's a dear little bird!" called one of the girls.

"Do another one!"

The dear little bird appeared to fly off. In its place was a lumpy shape with big pointy ears and long thin fingers.

"What's that?" The girls sounded puzzled.

"Stand sideways, Cyrus," hissed Ben. "Then they'll see your teeth."

Cyrus shuffled round and opened his mouth as wide as he could. Now the shadow of his long fangs fell on the tent wall.

He flexed his sharp claws and gave a rumbling growl.

There was complete silence outside. Then they heard Jessica's voice. She sounded scared.

"Stop it, Max! I know it's you."

"It's working!" whispered Max. "Rufus – I reckon they're ready for your special power now."

"My pleasure." Rufus seemed to shrivel before their eyes. Then he grew tall and thin and his stone melted away to leave a big looming skeleton. His bony shadow jiggled eerily in the torchlight, fingers clawing at the canvas as if he were coming to get the girls.

"**ARGGGGHHHHHH!**" The sounds of screaming and running feet disappeared off towards the house.

"There they go!" said Max triumpantly.

"I think you'll agree that mine was a spook-tacular performance!" exclaimed Rufus, resuming his gargoyle shape.

"Spluttering gutterz," said Toby. "You were super scary."

"That'll teach them to invade our secret camp!" declared Max.

"Can we go on the bouncy castle now?" asked Barney eagerly.

Ben went out and peered through the trees. "The castle's clear," he reported. "But the enemy princesses are all in the lounge with their duvets and they'll see us."

"We'll have to wait until they're asleep," said Max.

The gargoylz groaned with disappointment.

"Let's play a game while we wait," suggested Ben.

"Dead Lionz! Dead Lionz!" Zack piped up.

"No chance," said Max. "You lot always win. You're too good at not moving."

"Theo isn't," said Cyrus. "His tail always twitches."

"Well, your ears always flicker," declared Theo.

"No they don't!"

"Yes they do!"

"Let's play Dinosaur Snap," said Ben quickly. "You each put a card down in turn and shout 'Snap!' if it matches the one underneath it."

"Snap!" growled Rufus immediately.

"I haven't given out the cards yet," said Ben.

As soon as the cards were dealt, the gargoylz took turns to put them down.

"Snap!" shouted Toby.

"Those cards don't match," said Max. "You've got a Pterodactyl and that's an Allosaurus."

"Snap!" yelled Bart.

"It wasn't your turn—" began Ben.

"Snap!"

"Snap!"

"Snap!"

All the gargoylz were yelling at the same time.

Then Zack jumped up and threw the cards into the air.

"This isn't working," groaned Ben.

"What else can we play?"

"No more games!" decided Max. "We need to take action if we want to go on the bouncy castle before we get sent to bed. Those pesky girls have got to go to sleep so they don't see us outside. Time for Secret Plan: Rock-a-bye Princesses. And I know just whose special gargoyle power will do the trick."

Ben's eyes lit up with mischief. "Cyrus can sing them to sleep!" he exclaimed. "Good thinking, Agent Black. Come on, Cyrus."

With a fierce grin, Cyrus jumped onto Ben's lap and tucked himself under his T-shirt. "Ready to go!" came his muffled voice.

"You'd better hurry up," warned Toby.

"Yes," grumbled Bart.

"We can't wait much longer to have a bounce."

Max and Ben stepped fearfully into the lounge and stared in horror at the ghastly scene in front of their eyes.

There was a long row of duvets on the floor, and the party princesses were running up and down, shrieking at the tops of their voices. They all still had their frilly dresses and tiaras on; some wore their nighties on top. Jessica was wearing her pyjama bottoms as a cloak and a lampshade for a crown.

Max's mum sat slumped in a chair reading a bedtime story. No one was listening.

"Shall I start my song?" came a growly voice above the din.

"Not yet, Cyrus," Max whispered. "We've got to get Mum out of the room first."

One of Jessica's friends looked at Ben's bulging tummy and started to giggle. "He's had too much cake!" she told her friends.

Soon Ben was surrounded by a group of squealing princesses, all prodding his tummy.

"Let's go," he whispered to Max. "Before Cyrus is discovered."

The boys bounded away up the stairs. Max stopped at his bedroom door and staggered back in shock. His bed was piled high with girly coats and cardigans. But – even worse – someone had thrown a pair of sparkly shoes onto the pile and pink

glitter had got all
over his duvet.

"I shall never
sleep in here
again!" he croaked.
"My room's been
girlified!"

"That's perfect!"
exclaimed Ben eagerly.

"Perfect?" gasped Max.
"How would you like to wake up
in the morning covered in pink glitter?"

"That's not what I meant, Agent
Black," said Ben. "It's the perfect excuse
to get your mum out of the lounge. As
soon as she comes up here to see what's
happened, I'll go back down so Cyrus can
sing the girls to sleep."

"You're right! That's the answer, Agent
Neal!" Max stuck his head out of the
door. "MUM!" he yelled. "Emergency!
Something terrible's happened."

Mrs Black was soon upstairs, anxiously poking her head round the door. As Ben slipped back downstairs, Max showed her his glittery bed. "Disaster area," he wailed.

"Is that all?" said his mum. Brushing the glitter off the bed, she turned to go back down. But Max had to keep her upstairs for a few more minutes. Cyrus might not have got all the girls to sleep yet.

"You can't go!" he said, grabbing her arm. "The floor's all glittery now too. I'll get girly feet."

"I haven't got time to hoover tonight," sighed Mum. "I've got to settle Jessica and her friends down – somehow."

She headed for the stairs. Max tore after her. He could hear a few notes of a beautiful lullaby wafting out of the lounge door. Then there was silence.

When Max's mum reached the lounge, she gave a gasp. Max's heart missed a beat. Had she seen Cyrus?

He risked a peek. There, stretched out on their duvets, lay the princesses. Every one of them was sound asleep. Ben sat in a chair, reading the last page of a yucky fairy story out loud. Max saw that he had pink paper napkins stuck in his ears so that he wouldn't hear Cyrus's song.

"Thank you, Ben dear," said Mrs Black. "You must have cast a spell on them."

Ben gave Max's mum his best innocent smile. "A lullaby helped as well," he said sweetly.

Max stifled a giggle.

Mrs Black went off to the kitchen and came back with a huge tub of mint choc chip ice cream. She plonked it into Ben's hands.

"That's a thank-you for getting the girls to sleep," she said. "Sleep tight, boys."

"Awesome!" Ben sighed happily.

Then he felt the tub being snatched away from him.

"That's mine, I think," said Cyrus cheekily as he scampered off with it into the garden.

Five minutes later the tub of ice cream was empty and the boys and the gargoylz were all licking their lips.

"Last one on the bouncy castle is a turnip!" shouted Rufus. The gargoylz raced over and scrambled on. With every bounce they threw themselves at the pink walls, chuckling and whooping.

"I haven't had so much fun since we put springs in the vicar's slipperz and he bumped his head on the ceiling," called Toby. "Come and join us, boyz!"

Max and Ben stood and looked at the pink turrets and painted roses.

"I can't," said Max with a shudder.

"Nor can I," said Ben, making a face. "It's so revolting and girly."

"Shut your eyes then," said Barney. "That way you won't see what colour it is."

"That's the answer!" said Max. "Thanks, Barney."

The boys screwed up their eyes as tightly as they could and jumped onto the bouncy castle.

"We are bold ghost hunters," yelled Max happily as he was buffeted from side to side by the gargoylz, "and this is the dreaded Terror Towers, the most haunted castle in the world."

"Its dungeons are full of howling spooks," added Ben, bouncing blindly off the walls, "and its spiky

portcullis is ready to drop on enemy invaders."

The gargoylz set up an unearthly howling while Rufus turned into a clattering skeleton.

"But there's nothing to be scared of," called Max happily, "as long as we don't open our eyes!"

Gargoylz Fact File

Full name: Tobias the Third
Known as: Toby
Special Power: Flying
Likes: All kinds of pranks and mischief – especially playing jokes on the vicar
Dislikes: Mrs Hogsbottom, garden gnomes

Full name: Barnabas
Known as: Barney
Special Power: Making big stinks!
Likes: Cookiez
Dislikes: Being surprised by humanz

Name: Eli
Special Power: Turning into a grass snake
Likes: Sssports Day, Ssslithering
Dislikes: Ssscary ssstories

Full name: Bartholomew

Known as: Bart

Special Power: Burping spiders

Likes: Being grumpy

Dislikes: Being told to cheer up

Full name: Theophilus

Known as: Theo

Special Power: Turning into a ferocious tiger (well, tabby kitten!)

Likes: Sunny spots and cosy places

Dislikes: Rain

Full name: Zackary

Known as: Zack

Special Power: Making himself invisible to humanz

Likes: Bouncing around, eating bramblz, thistlz, and anything with Pricklz!

Dislikes: Keeping still

Name: Azzan
Special POWer: Breathing fir
Likes: Surprises
Dislikes: Smoke going up his nose and making him sneeze

Name: Ira
Special Power: Making it rain
Likes: Making humanz walk the plank
Dislikes: Being bored

Name: Cyrus
Special Power: Singing lullabies to send humanz to sleep
Likes: Fun dayz out
Dislikes: Snoring

Name: Rufus
Special Power: Turning into a skeleton
Likes: Playing spooky tricks
Dislikes: Squeezing into small spaces